KV-048-705

The Easter Kitty Bunny

Grab your magical cat ears and join Gabby and the Gabby Cats for an adventure in the dollhouse!

3/05/24
15/10/24

mx

WITHDRAWN

Books should be returned or renewed by the last
date above. Renew by phone **03000 41 31 31** or
online *www.kent.gov.uk/libs*

Libraries Registration & Archives

C334968809

ORCHARD BOOKS

First published in Great Britain in 2024 by Hodder & Stoughton

DreamWorks Gabby's Dollhouse © 2024 DreamWorks Animation LLC. All Rights Reserved

A CIP catalogue record for this book is available from the British Library

ISBN 978 1 40837 178 7

1 3 5 7 9 10 8 6 4 2

Printed and bound in China

Orchard Books
An imprint of Hachette Children's Group
part of Hodder & Stoughton Limited
Carmelite House
50 Victoria Embankment
London EC4Y 0DZ
An Hachette UK Company
www.hachette.co.uk
www.hachettechildrens.co.uk

Happy Easter!

An egg-stra special Dollhouse Delivery arrived.

"I wonder if it's an Easter surprise," said Gabby.

It was! Gabby pulled out a little Easter basket with a teeny-tiny egg inside.
Whoa – the egg was wiggling!

Maybe Kitty Fairy could help figure out what was inside.

"It's time to get tiny!" Gabby said.

Gabby and Pandy Paws brought the wiggly egg to the Fairy Tail Garden.

"I've never seen an egg like this before," said Kitty Fairy.

"Is it hatching yet?" asked Pandy Paws .

"Not yet," Kitty Fairy replied. "But it looks like it's getting close."

CatRat popped up from underneath the basket and accidentally knocked it over.

"Did someone say 'egg'? I'm ready for breakfast!" he shouted.

Uh-oh! The egg started rolling away.

"Gotcha!" CatRat said as he popped up from a different hidey-hole. The egg balanced on top of his head. But before Gabby could reach it, the egg rolled down the slide.

Cakey Cat was in the kitchen decorating Easter eggs. They looked like spring fruits and vegetables. He didn't see the egg roll off the slide and on to the platter.

"Oops! I didn't finish decorating you," Cakey said when he saw the egg. He painted the egg and placed it back on the platter.

"Hi, Cakey. Did you see an egg roll in here?" Pandy asked.

"The only eggs I see are my Easter garden eggs," Cakey said. "I've just finished decorating them."

"One of these eggs must be ours," Gabby said.

"How are we going to find it?" Pandy asked.

"I don't know yet, but let's think," Gabby replied. "We know our egg was orange, so it must be one of the carrot eggs. I bet MerCat can use some spa science to help us figure out which one is about to hatch."

Pandy and Gabby took the basket of carrot eggs to MerCat.

"Can you help us?" Gabby asked.

"You came to the right mermaid scientist," MerCat said, smiling.

MerCat pulled out a vase filled with water. Then she added a special sink-float potion. The water shimmered and shone.

"If you drop the eggs into the water one at a time, only yours will sink," MerCat said.

Gabby put the first egg in the water. It floated. That one wasn't it.

Pandy tried next. He couldn't watch. Finally, it sank. That one was the egg!

"There's nothing a little spa science can't figure out," said MerCat proudly.

Gabby and Pandy Paws took the egg to the bedroom next. Pillow Cat had the perfect springtime story to share while they waited for the egg to hatch.

In the story, Easter Pandy hid eggs for his friends to find.
Can you find the hidden eggs?

When Easter Pandy tried to
hide the last egg, it wiggled. So,
Easter Pandy wiggled, too. Then
they had a dance-off!

The egg wiggled while they were listening to the story.

"I think the egg really likes that story," Gabby said.

"Maybe we can get it to wiggle some more – right out of its shell!" said Pandy Paws.

They went to the music room together to see DJ Catnip.

DJ Catnip found some egg shakers to help them wiggle.
Then they danced. CatRat joined in, too. Everyone wiggled
and danced – even the egg!

Then the egg began to hatch. It was the moment they'd been waiting for! What could be inside?

It was a springtime kitty
bunny! She said her name was

Eggie

Everyone was so excited to meet her.

They took Eggie to the Fairy Tail Garden to meet
Kitty Fairy and show her around.

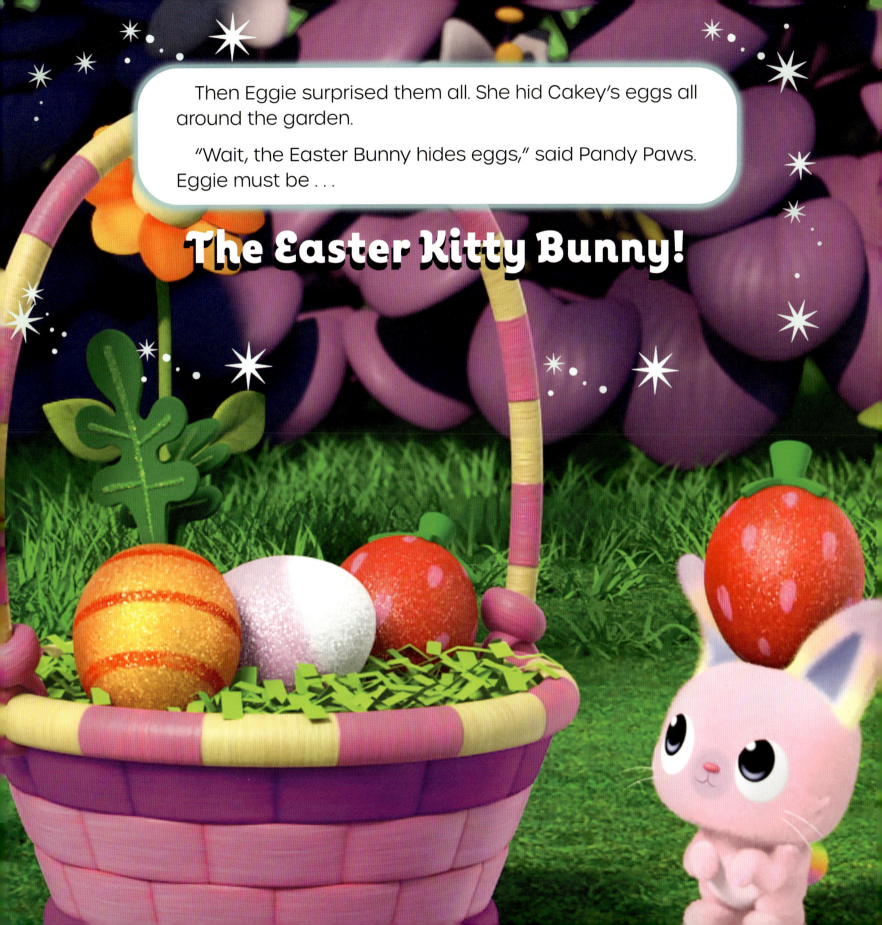

Then Eggie surprised them all. She hid Cakey's eggs all around the garden.

"Wait, the Easter Bunny hides eggs," said Pandy Paws. Eggie must be . . .

The Easter Kitty Bunny!

Kitty Fairy used garden magic to make everyone Easter baskets.
Then, they all searched for hidden eggs. Can you help find the eggs?

Now Gabby has her very own Easter Kitty Bunny. What a cat-tastic surprise!

Are you ready for a surprise?
You get to pick the Gabby Cat of the Day!
Choose a Gabby Cat and make up a song for them.